Written by

Doug Peterson

Illustrated by

Greg Hardin and Robert Vann

ZONDERVAN.COM/
AUTHORTRACKER

www.bigidea.com

www.zonderkidz.com

LarryBoy and the Mudslingers
Copyright © 2006 by Big Idea, Inc.
Illustrations copyright © 2006 by Big Idea, Inc.

Requests for information should be addressed to:
Zonderkidz, Grand Rapids, Michigan 49530

Library of Congress Cataloging-in-Publication Data

Peterson, Doug.
    Larryboy and the mudslingers! / by Doug Peterson.
        p. cm.
    "Big Idea."
    Summary: A mud-balloon fight--orchestrated by the dastardly Big Apple--threatens
to destroy the city until Larryboy figures out that the key to stopping the fighting lies
in forgiving one another.
    ISBN-13: 978-0-310-71149-0 (hardcover)
    ISBN-10: 0-310-71149-5 (hardcover)
    [1. Forgiveness--Fiction. 2. Revenge--Fiction. 3. Mud--Fiction. 4. Heroes--Fiction. 5.
Christian life--Fiction.] I. Title: Mudslingers!. II. Title.
    PZ7.P44334Latm 2006
    [E]--dc22

                                                                    2005032138

Written by Doug Peterson
Illustrations by Greg Hardin and Robert Vann
Editors: Karen Poth and Amy DeVries
Interior Design and Art Direction: Ron Eddy

Printed in China

05 06 07 08 • 5 4 3 2 1

"Forgive us our sins, as we also forgive
everyone who sins against us.
Keep us from falling into sin when we are tempted."

(Luke 11:4)

A Lesson in Forgiveness

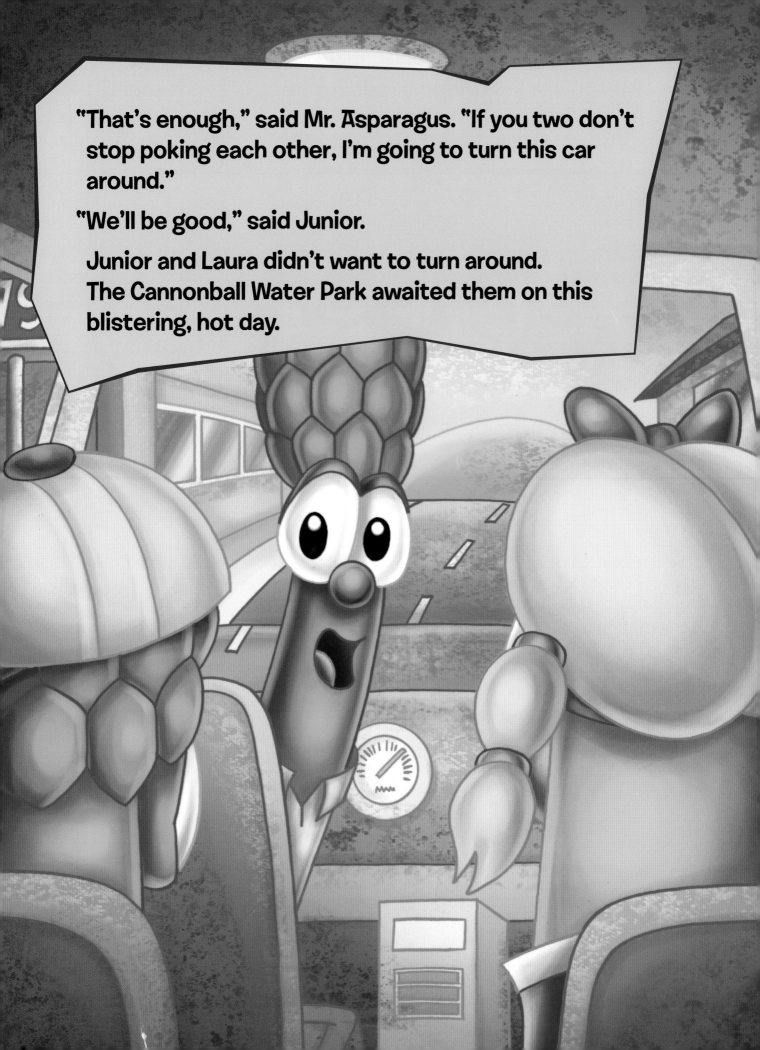

"That's enough," said Mr. Asparagus. "If you two don't stop poking each other, I'm going to turn this car around."

"We'll be good," said Junior.

Junior and Laura didn't want to turn around. The Cannonball Water Park awaited them on this blistering, hot day.

Bad Apple's sidekick, Curly,
looked up from his dinner of dirt.

"How will we strike back?" he asked.

"With our secret weapon!" declared the Bad Apple.

Then, with a sinister laugh, the Bad Apple poured water
onto Curly's plate, turning the dirt into sticky goo.

"We'll trap them in the mud."

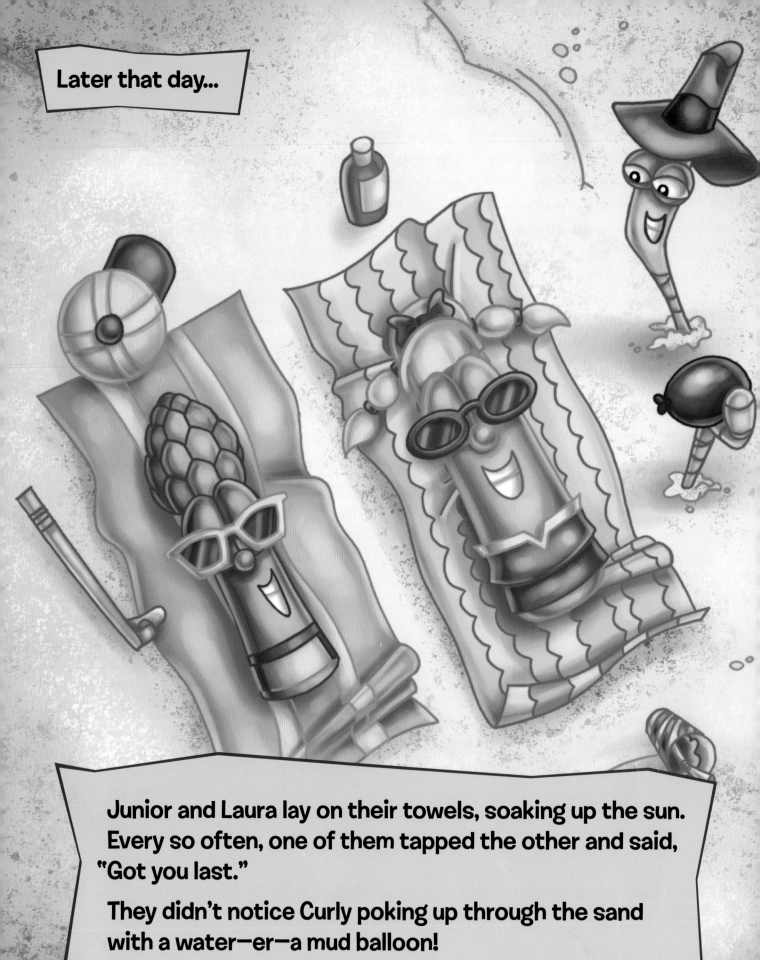

Later that day...

Junior and Laura lay on their towels, soaking up the sun. Every so often, one of them tapped the other and said, "Got you last."

They didn't notice Curly poking up through the sand with a water—er—a mud balloon!

He hurled the gooshy balloon high into the air. Down it came...

SPLURT! ...right on Laura's head.

"What did you do that for?" Laura hollered at Junior.

Junior's eyes popped open. But before he could say, "I didn't do it," Laura picked up another one of Curly's balloons.

"I can play dirty too!" she growled.

SPLOT!

"Got you last!"

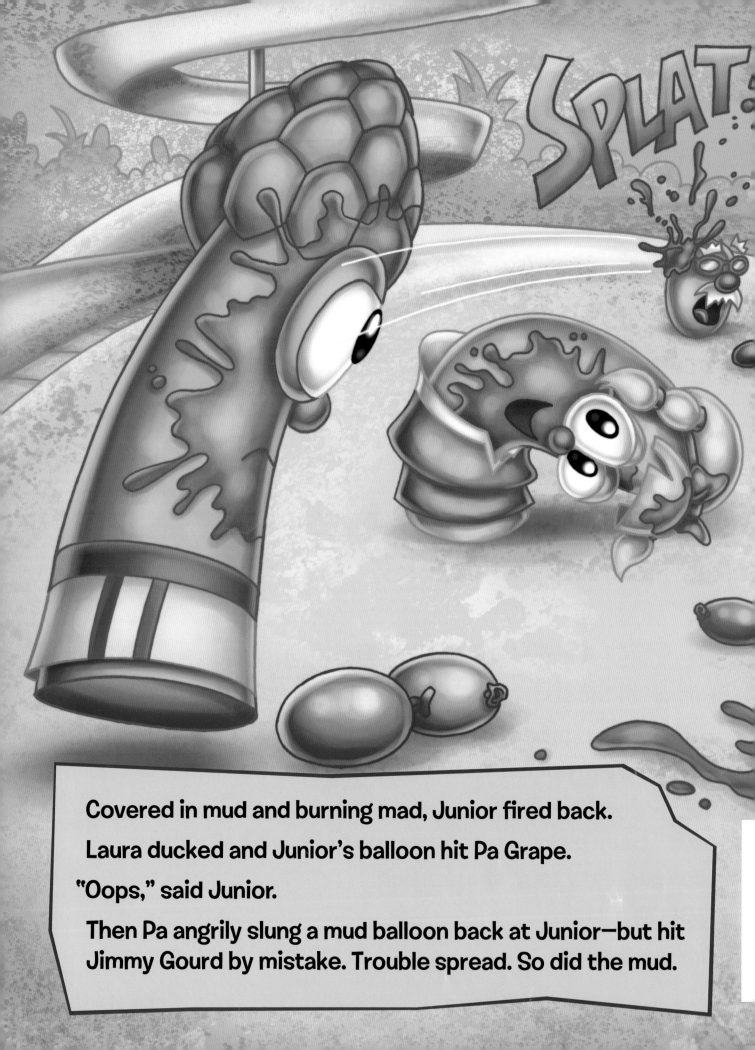

Covered in mud and burning mad, Junior fired back.

Laura ducked and Junior's balloon hit Pa Grape.

"Oops," said Junior.

Then Pa angrily slung a mud balloon back at Junior—but hit Jimmy Gourd by mistake. Trouble spread. So did the mud.

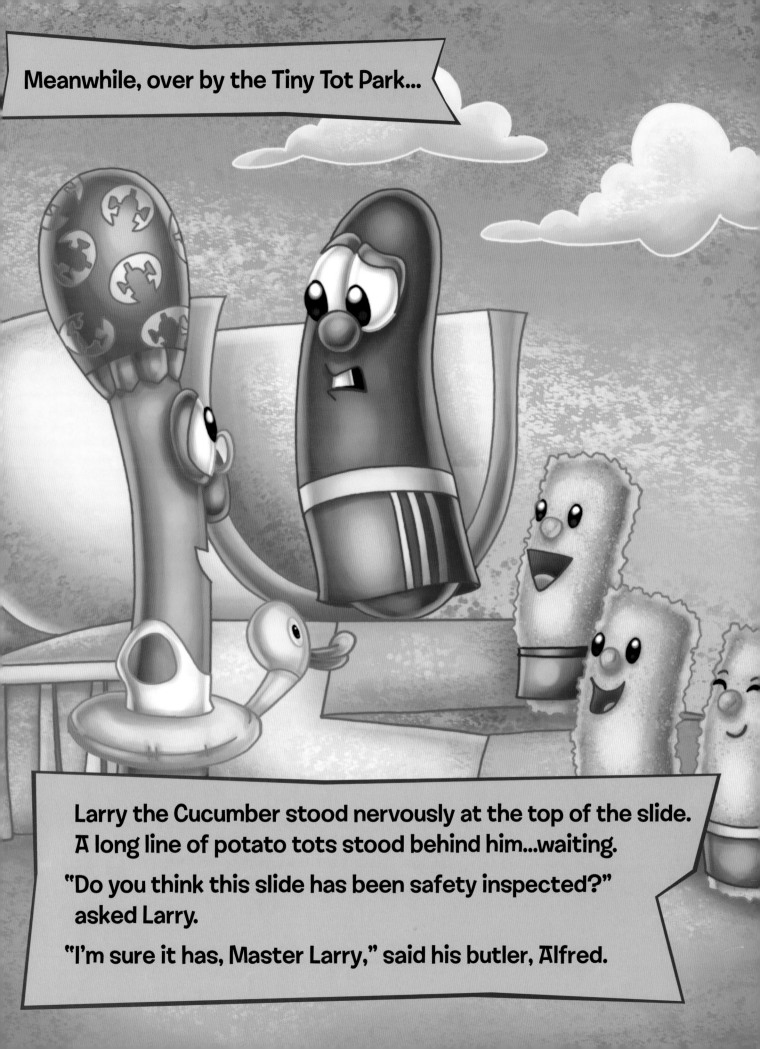

Meanwhile, over by the Tiny Tot Park...

Larry the Cucumber stood nervously at the top of the slide. A long line of potato tots stood behind him...waiting.

"Do you think this slide has been safety inspected?" asked Larry.

"I'm sure it has, Master Larry," said his butler, Alfred.

Suddenly, Larry heard a wild commotion on the sundeck. He glanced over and saw Mayor Blueberry zing a mud balloon at Petunia. Then Petunia threw a balloon at Bob the Tomato.

"Duty calls!" cried Larry. He turned and jostled his way back through the line of small potatoes.

"That's the fifth time today he's chickened out of going down the slide," mumbled one tot.

Larry leaped into the changing room.
He reappeared as LarryBoy, the Purple Protector!

Soon, LarryBoy was holding a mud balloon too.

"Don't do it, LarryBoy!" pleaded Alfred.

But LarryBoy hurled the balloon at Scooter. The balloon bounced off a stack of inner tubes and smacked Alfred instead!

Alfred scraped the mud off his monocle and studied it. "This is strange," he said. "The mud is super sticky. It won't come off, even with water."

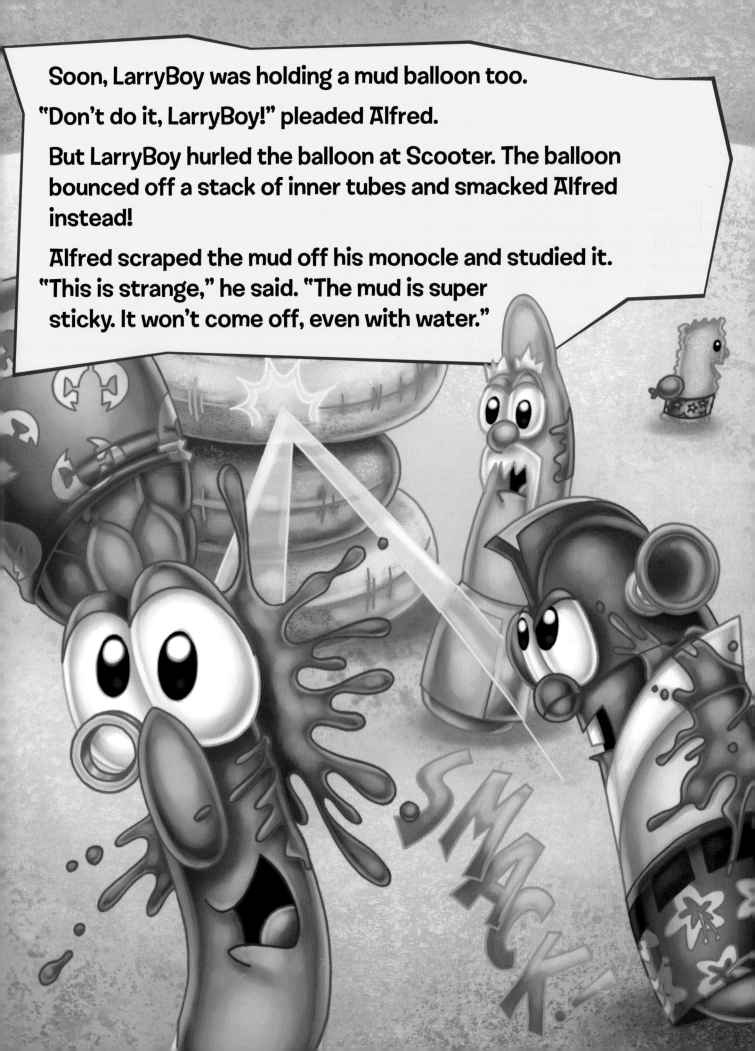

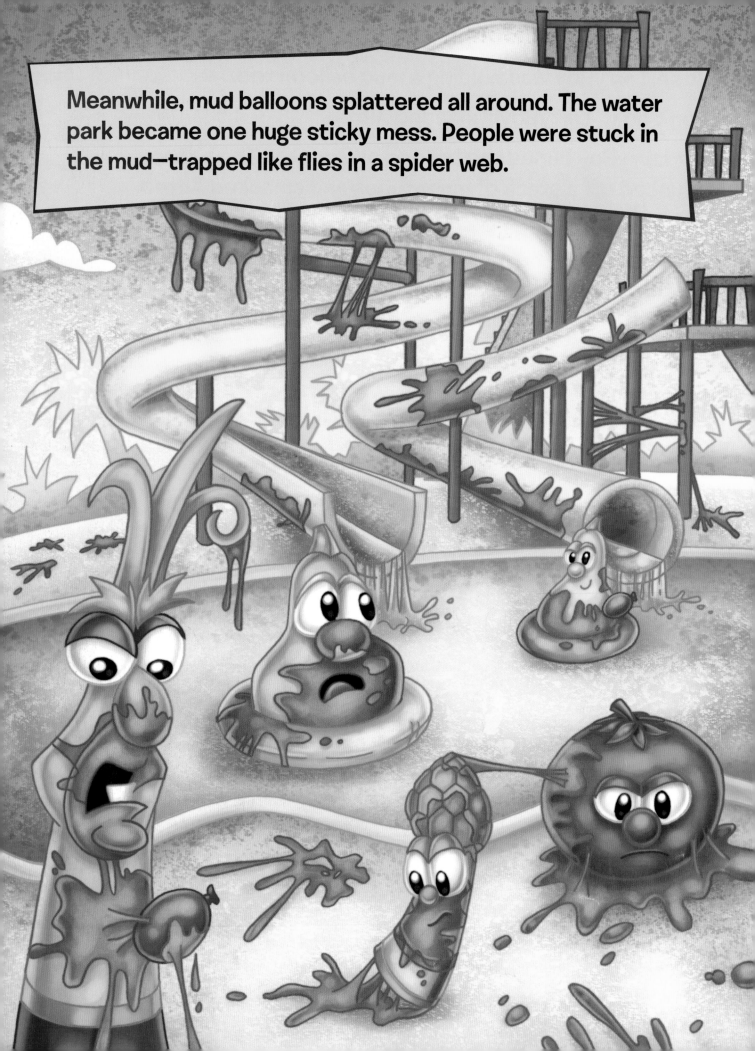

Meanwhile, mud balloons splattered all around. The water park became one huge sticky mess. People were stuck in the mud—trapped like flies in a spider web.

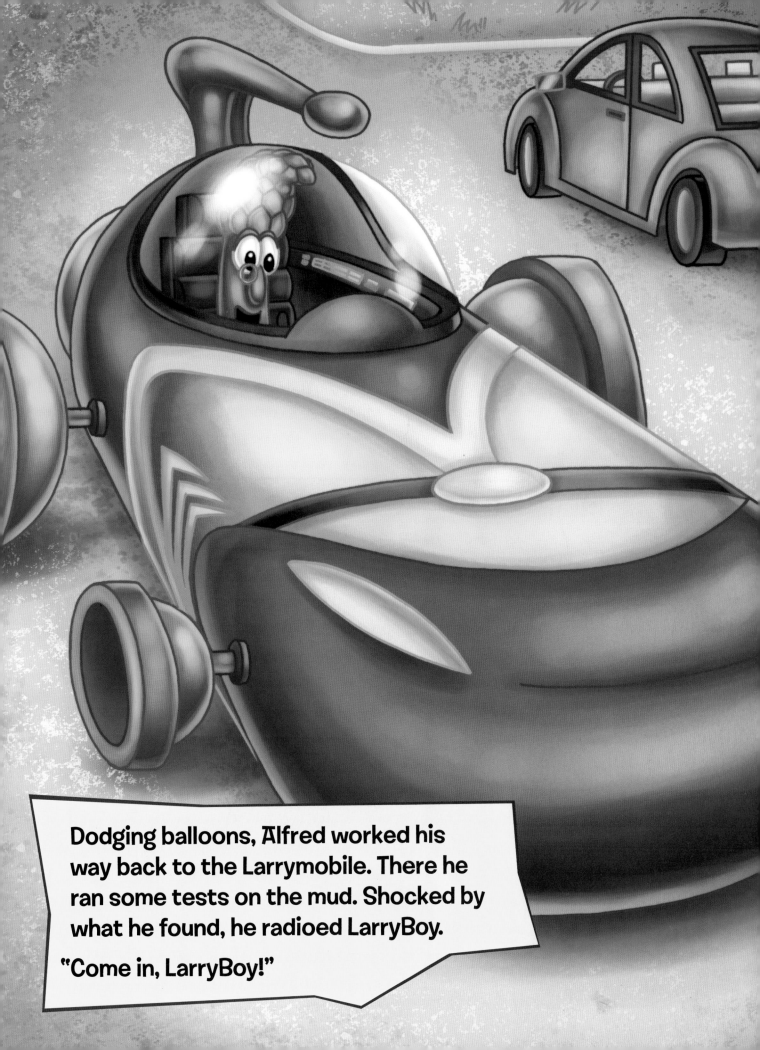

Dodging balloons, Alfred worked his way back to the Larrymobile. There he ran some tests on the mud. Shocked by what he found, he radioed LarryBoy.

"Come in, LarryBoy!"

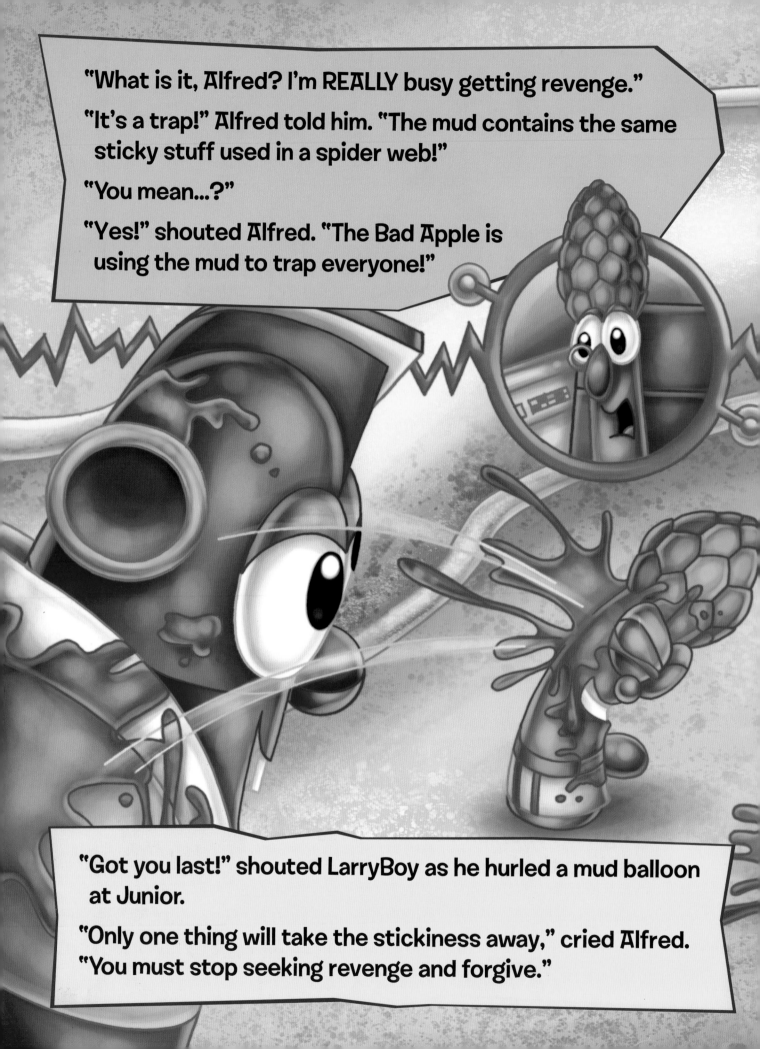

"What is it, Alfred? I'm REALLY busy getting revenge."

"It's a trap!" Alfred told him. "The mud contains the same sticky stuff used in a spider web!"

"You mean...?"

"Yes!" shouted Alfred. "The Bad Apple is using the mud to trap everyone!"

"Got you last!" shouted LarryBoy as he hurled a mud balloon at Junior.

"Only one thing will take the stickiness away," cried Alfred. "You must stop seeking revenge and forgive."

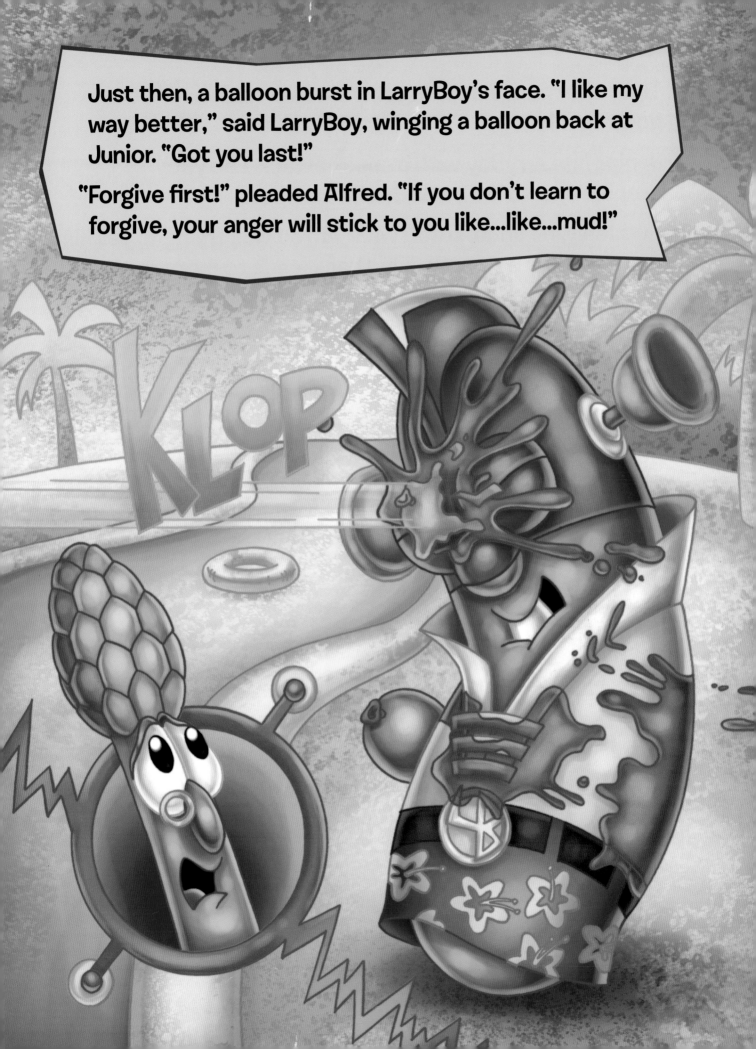

The water park was a disaster. People squirmed in the gooey gunk.

Junior hit LarryBoy with a sneak attack. LarryBoy prepared to strike back. But he stopped.

Suddenly, he understood what Alfred was trying to tell him. Revenge was a trap. Striking back leads to more revenge...

...more anger...and more mud.

With that, LarryBoy spoke these heroic words:
"I'm sorry, Junior! Can you forgive me?"

Instantly, the mud on LarryBoy's super suit lost its sticky power. A little splash of water washed the mud away.

Curly and the Bad Apple continued to sling mud.
But no one in the crowd returned fire.

The Bad Apple grumbled, "Foiled again!"

"To the water slide!" Petunia shouted.

Everyone took turns zipping down the Screaming Water Slide.
The cool, clear water washed away their mud and anger.

Even LarryBoy decided to go down the slide—the Tiny Tot Slide, that is.

"What if my mask flies off?" he asked nervously.

"The slide is only five feet long," said Alfred, rolling his eyes. "Take the plunge." As LarryBoy tried to work up the courage, a tiny tater tot wobbled up from behind...and gave him a nudge.

LarryBoy raced down the slide. "That was great!" he shouted.

"Got you last!" joked the little tot.